A Treasury of
Children's
CLASSICS

Commissioning Editor   Christine Deverell
Additional Illustrations   Richard Deverell
Design   Ian Jones

©2000 Robert Frederick Limited
4-5 North Parade
Bath, U.K.
BA1 1LF

A Treasury of
Children's
CLASSICS

THREE FAIRY TALES

Adapted by

CHRISTINE DEVERELL

· C O N T E N T S ·

Puss in Boots

ILLUSTRATED BY JAN NESBITT

Once upon a time there lived a poor miller who had three sons. When he died, all he owned was divided between his sons; the eldest had the mill, the second son had the donkey and cart, and all that was left for the youngest son was the miller's black cat.

The boy was very fond of the cat, but could not see how she would ever make his fortune.

As he stroked her gently, she said, "Don't worry, master. If you do what I tell you, you will see what I can do for you. First, get me a large bag and a pair of boots." The miller's son took the last few shillings he had, and bought the cat a large bag and a pair of yellow boots.

The cat put on her new boots and went out into the garden. She picked some lettuce and put it in the new bag. Then off she went across the fields until she found a rabbit hole. She put the bag down with its mouth wide open so the lettuce could be seen. Then she hid herself behind a low hedge. Soon, a fat grey rabbit popped his head out of the hole. He smelt the fresh lettuce and jumped into the bag to eat it.

Puss-in-Boots immediately leapt from behind the hedge and swiftly drew the strings of the bag together and the fat rabbit was caught.

Then Puss slung the bag over her shoulder and set off in her yellow boots until she came to the King's palace. She presented herself to the King, and bowing low said, "Your Majesty, I have brought you a fat rabbit from the estate of my master, the Marquis of Carabas." The King was amused at the sight of a black cat in yellow boots, but he graciously accepted the gift.

The next day Puss put a handful of grain into her bag and went out to the fields. She set the bag as before and lay down beside it pretending to be dead.

11

This time two pheasants came and started to eat the grain. She waited for the right moment, and quickly gathered up the strings of the bag, catching both birds inside. Once more she set off for the palace, and presented herself to the King.

"My master, the Marquis of Carabas, begs your acceptance of these two pheasants," said Puss-in Boots, bowing gracefully. "Tell your master," said the King, "that I am pleased to accept his gift. He must have a very fine estate." "Oh indeed, it is, very fine," said Puss as she bowed and took her leave of the King.

As she passed through the great halls, she heard that the King and his daughter were going to drive beside the river that afternoon. Puss raced home to her master, and told him about her visit to the palace, and then commanded him,

"I want you to go and swim in the river and if anyone asks your name, you are to say that you are the Marquis of Carabas." So he left Puss-in-Boots to guard his clothes and went and swam in the river.

Puss carefully hid the clothes under a pile of stones, and waited for the royal carriage. As it approached, Puss ran out, shouting, "Help! Help! The Marquis of Carabas is drowning!" The King ordered the coach to stop and sent his servants to rescue the Marquis. Then Puss went up to the carriage, and with his hat in his hand, bowed to the King and Princess and said, "We are indeed so grateful that you happened to be passing just now. But, alas, a thief has stolen my master's clothes."

13

The King sent a servant to the palace to get a suit, and when the miller's son put it on, he looked just like a prince. "This is my master, the Marquis of Carabas," said Puss to the King and Princess as she graciously introduced him.

"We hope you will drive on and dine with the Marquis." "It will be a pleasure," replied the King, and he invited the Marquis to ride in his carriage.

Puss ran ahead of the carriage and took a short cut across the fields. Back on the road, she came across some haymakers.

They stared at the sight of a black cat in yellow boots, and she told them sternly,

"When the King passes this way and asks to whom this field of hay belongs, you are to say, 'To the Marquis of Carabas, your Majesty.' If you don't, you will be chopped into little pieces."

Then she ran on until she came to a field where reapers were busy cutting the wheat. "When the King passes this way," said Puss, "and asks to whom this field of wheat belongs, you are to say, 'To the Marquis of Carabas, your Majesty.' If you don't, you will chopped into little pieces."

Now the land really belonged to a terrible Ogre, and Puss-in-Boots carried on running until she reached his great castle.

No one ever visited him because he was so frightening, but when he opened the door, Puss walked straight in, showing off her fine boots.

The Ogre was so shocked that he could only stare at her. "I have heard that you can turn yourself into a wild beast; is that true?" said Puss, calmly. "Well naturally." said the Ogre swelling with pride, and then in a flash he became a roaring lion.

Poor Puss ran and hid herself up the chimney! The Ogre changed himself back again and laughed at Puss, who said, "It is truly wonderful that an Ogre such as yourself can become a great lion, but I very much doubt that you could change into a tiny creature, say, a mouse?"

"Pooh! no problem at all," said the Ogre, and in an instant he had disappeared and Puss saw a tiny mouse running across the room.

She pounced and seized the creature, and with one shake, the Ogre was dead.

17

At this moment, the King's carriage drew up outside the castle. "You have a splendid estate," said the King to the miller's son, for sure enough, the haymakers and reapers had obeyed Puss, and told him the land belonged to the Marquis of Carabas; "And this is a magnificent castle." They went inside and sat down to a feast.

"This young man would make a good husband for my daughter," thought the King. "Your title does not match your wealth. I shall make you a Prince." The Princess loved the Prince, and he loved her.

So they were married, and lived together happily in the Ogre's castle. Puss-in Boots lived in comfort to the end of her life and she never had to hunt again.

Rumpelstiltskin

ILLUSTRATED BY STEPHEN ANGEL

Once there was a poor miller who had a very beautiful daughter. He was so poor, he couldn't pay his taxes, and when the King threatened to put him in prison, the miller in desperation said, "I have a daughter who can spin gold out of straw."

"Then bring her to me immediately," ordered the King. The frightened girl was led to a room which was filled with a huge pile of straw.

"Spin all this into gold before morning, or you will be punished." She pleaded to be excused, for she knew that she was

not able to spin gold out of straw, but it was no use. The door was locked and she sat there alone and wept.

After a while, the door opened and in walked a little man. "Why are you sad?" he asked.

24

"The King has ordered me to spin all this straw into gold, and I don't know how to do it."

"What will you give me if I do it for you?" said the little man. The girl gave him her necklace, and he sat down to

work, spinning the straw into fine gold. By morning he was
finished. The King was delighted with what he saw, but he
wanted more. So he took the miller's daughter to a larger room
filled with straw and told her to spin it into gold by the next
morning. Again she sat down and wept.

Soon, the little man came into the room and said, "What
will you give me if I do this for you?" She gave him her gold
ring, and he worked until morning, when the task was complete.

The King was greedy and wanted even more gold, so the
next evening he took the girl to an even larger room,
filled to the rafters with straw. He said,
"If you can do this tonight, you
will be my wife."

26

The little man came in as before and asked her, "What will you give me to spin all this into gold for you?" She despaired, for she had nothing left to give him.

"Then promise me," said the little man, "your first child when you are queen."

The miller's daughter could only agree to give the little man what he wanted though she hoped that she would never have to keep her promise. The little man spun a huge pile of gold, and not a piece of straw was left. In the morning the King found all he wanted, and the miller's daughter became his Queen.

A year passed, and the Queen gave birth to a lovely daughter. She was so happy that she forgot about the funny little man and the promise she made. Until one day he appeared and reminded her of it.

She offered him all the treasure of the kingdom but he refused to accept it. She cried and cried because she could not bear to part with her little baby.

29

The little man gave in to her pleading saying, "Very well, I will give you three days, and if in that time you can guess my name, then you may keep your child." The Queen stayed up all night thinking of all the names she had ever heard and writing them down in a long list.

The next day, the little man came to her room and she began to work through the list. Peter, John, Mark, Isaac, Thomas, Henry, Jeremiah . . . But with every name she tried she received the same reply: "No! That's not my name."

On the second day she tried all the strangest names that she had heard of, and some that she made up herself, like Roofabeef, Gug and Boogie. But the little man just laughed and said, "You will never guess my name!" The Queen sent her servants out to see if they could discover any other names.

All but one returned with no new names for her. But late in the evening, as the remaining servant was making his way back to the castle, he heard a little man singing in the woods:

"Merrily the feast I'll make,
Today I'll brew, tomorrow bake;
Merrily I'll dance and sing,
For next day a stranger bring:
Little does my lady dream
Rumpelstiltskin is my name!"

32

This faithful servant told the Queen of his fortunate discovery, and when on the third day her little visitor arrived, she asked him, "Is your name William? "No."

"Is it Charles?" "No."

"Could it be . . . Rumpelstiltskin?"

"Who told you that? Who told you that?" cried the little man; and he shook his fists and stamped his feet so hard that he made a hole in the floor and fell right into it.

Moaning and groaning, he pulled himself out of the hole and ran away. The Queen lived happily with the King and her daughter, and they were never bothered by Rumpelstiltskin again.

Little Red Riding Hood

ILLUSTRATED BY DAVID LONG

A very long time ago, so many wild beasts prowled about in the forests that no one was ever surprised to meet a wolf or a bear. A little girl, whom everyone called Red Riding Hood, lived in a cottage on the edge of a wood with her mother and father, who worked as a woodcutter. Red Riding Hood was not her real name, but it was given her because she always wore a red hooded coat that her grandmother had made for her.

Now this grandmother lived alone in a rose covered cottage on the other side of the wood, and Red Riding Hood loved to visit her. One day little girl's mother called her and said, "Why don't you go to your grandmother's house for tea today? She has not been well, so I have baked her a cake and made her some lemonade." Handing her the gifts in a basket she added, "Do not stray from the path and do not stop to talk to anyone on the way."

Red Riding Hood promised to go straight to the cottage; so her mother tied on her red hood, kissed her goodbye, and off she went.

She had not gone very far along the path when she met a wolf. "Good morning, Little Red Riding Hood, where are you

going today?" he asked her. "Good morning Mr Wolf" she said, politely, "I am going to visit my grandmother." "And what are you carrying in the basket?" asked the wolf.

"Cake and lemonade for our tea," Little Red Riding Hood replied. "So where does your grandmother live?" asked the wolf

in his sweetest voice. "I continue along this path, take the left path when it divides in two, and walk for another ten minutes.

It's the cottage that is covered with roses." "Aha, your grandmother likes flowers, does she? Why don't you pick some of these from beside the path and take them to her?" suggested the wolf.

Then the wolf trotted off, and Little Red Riding Hood thought it would be a great idea to gather a posy for her grandmother.

First, she picked a few flowers from beside the path, but then she saw that there were some prettier ones under the trees. So she disobeyed her mother's command, and stepped off the path.

The sun was shining through the branches and birds were singing happily. Little Red Riding Hood suddenly remembered that she should have kept to the path and gone straight to her grandmother's cottage, so she picked up her basket and the bunch of flowers, and set off once again.

Meanwhile, the wolf had raced ahead, following Little Red Riding Hood's directions to the cottage. "The rose covered cottage, she said,   so this must be it. Aha!"he said to himself, "Now I shall gobble up the old grandmother, and I'll have Little Red Riding Hood for dessert." He knocked on the door very gently. "Lift the latch and come in." said the old lady. The wolf lifted the latch and burst

through the door, and gobbled up the poor old grandmother in

one mouthful. Then he found one of her big frilly nightcaps in a drawer, pulled it over his ears and jumped into bed, taking care to draw the sheet well up under his chin. A few moments later Red Riding Hood tapped on the door of the cottage.

"Lift the latch and come in," said the wolf in his softest voice. But this voice did not sound like Little Red Riding Hood's grandmother, and the little girl wondered what was wrong. "Mother

has sent some cake and lemonade for our tea, but grandmother, how strange your voice sounds, and why are you in bed?"

"I have a cold on my chest," answered the wolf. "Come here, my dear and sit on the bed." As Red Riding Hood approached the bed, she could not believe what she saw.

"Oh Grandmother, what big eyes you have!" she said.

"All the better to see you with my dear," answered the wolf.

"But Grandmother, what big ears you have."

"All the better to hear you with, my dear."

"But Grandmother, what big teeth you have."

"All the better to gobble you up with my dear," said the wolf as he leapt out of the bed.

Little Red Riding Hood turned and ran screaming towards the door.

The wolf had just caught her red cloak in his mouth when the door burst open, and Little Red Riding Hood's own father came rushing in.

With one blow of his axe he struck the wicked wolf dead, and picked up Little Red Riding Hood in his arms and hugged her.

"Oh Father, I think the wolf must have eaten up dear Grandmother," sobbed Little Red Riding Hood. So he took out his knife, and carefully cut the wolf open. Inside, they found the old Grandmother safe and sound, for the wolf in his greed had swallowed her whole, and his teeth had not touched her.

They all sat down to enjoy their cake and lemonade, and
Little Red Riding Hood promised that she would never talk to
any wolf that she might meet in the woods, and she would
always obey her mother and never stray from the path.

48